EMERGENCY IN ESCAPE POD FOUR

Welcome to the

Universe

Star Wars Journals

The Fight for Justice by Luke Skywalker

Hero for Hire by Han Solo

Captive to Evil by Princess Leia Organa

Star Wars Science Adventures

#1 Emergency in Escape Pod Four

#2 Journey Across Planet X

EMERGENCY IN ESCAPE POD FOUR

Jude Watson and K·D· Burkett

SCHOLASTIC INC.
New York Toronto London Auckland Sydney
Mexico City New Delhi Hong Kong

Special thanks to John Lawrence and Ed Campion of Johnson Space Center/NASA. Thanks also to Laura Allen and Super Science *magazine for the Rocket Fuel activity on page 82.*

Interior art by Frank Boyd Forney

ISBN 0-590-20227-8

12 11 10 9 8 7 6 5 4 3 2 1   9/9 0 1 2 3 4/0

Printed in the U.S.A.

First Scholastic printing, February 1999

PROLOGUE

The escape pod careened through space. It turned over and over, faster and faster, like a laserball tossed by an angry Wookiee.

Inside the pod, the astromech droid Artoo-Detoo beeped frantically.

"No, I *can't* get to the controls, Artoo," his fellow droid, See-Threepio, said. "As you can see, I'm on the ceiling."

Artoo whistled.

"I'm not letting go of this handle," Threepio answered. "I'm not built for this kind of travel, you know. My circuits will get smashed to bits! Perhaps one of our other passengers can pilot."

"I'm not programmed for piloting," Forbee-X, a research droid, answered.

"And I can't seem to push away from this wall," twelve-year-old Stuart Zissu answered. "It's like I'm tied up with invisible rope."

"Artoo, this is all your fault," Threepio scolded, looking down at his friend. "You're the one who told Princess Leia we would go on this mission."

Artoo beeped and whirred.

"No, I did *not* volunteer!" Threepio insisted. "My memory circuits are in perfect working condition, despite the terrible banging they are receiving. I remember every detail of how we got into this mess. . . ."

COUNTDOWN

Lush green vines covered the hangar opening at the Rebel base on Yavin 4. It was early morning, but already the steamy air felt heavy. The space pilots hurried about their business. They tried to ignore the heat.

See-Threepio extended his finger joints and then contracted them. "There's one good thing about having to leave Yavin 4, Artoo," he said. "This jungle moon is simply *terrible* for my joint connectors."

Artoo responded with a long whistle and a short beep.

"I am *not* complaining," Threepio answered in a huff. "All this humid air could cause me to malfunction. If you had a shiny gold-plated exterior, you'd worry about your appearance, too."

"You two had better quit arguing and get

aboard," Luke Skywalker told them with a grin as he and Han Solo approached. "It's a long way to Delantine."

"At last, we'll get some peace and quiet around here," Han remarked gruffly. But he gave Artoo a friendly pat.

Just then, Princess Leia Organa approached. "All set for takeoff?" she asked.

"Did I say peace and quiet?" Solo said, rolling his eyes. "I *knew* I spoke too soon."

Leia ignored Solo. She knew that ignoring him would bother him more than anything else. She turned to the droids. "I want to thank you for volunteering for this mission," she told them.

"Volunteering?" Threepio asked, his hand fluttering near his chest-plate. He swiveled his head. His vision sensors stared down at Artoo.

"The destruction of the Death Star hasn't solved our problems," Leia continued, her face grim. "Now the Imperials have to convince the galaxy that they're still in charge. Every new mission will have its dangers. This one is no exception."

"But we're just escorting Trux Zissu to his new post on Delantine," Threepio stated. "It hardly sounds dangerous. He is going to govern the planet, not attack it."

"The Empire is determined to prevent Governor Zissu from reaching his post," Leia warned. "We know they are plotting to overthrow the Delantine government so they can control the planet."

"Artoo didn't tell me this," Threepio said. "Are you sure my diplomatic skills will be needed on this voyage? Perhaps a droid with defensive skills would be more appropriate, Princess Leia."

Artoo gave a low whistle.

"I am *not* being cowardly," Threepio insisted. "I'm simply suggesting that I might not be the best droid —"

"Threepio, there are sixteen different languages on Delantine," Leia interrupted. "Your skills *are* needed to help Governor Zissu get settled. And you promised me that you'd watch over his son Stuart as well." The princess sounded a little impatient. She didn't have time for doubts or second-guessing.

If there was one thing that overcame Threepio's natural timidity, it was his loyalty. "Of course, Princess Leia," he told her. "I'm ready to board."

"Have you seen Forbee-X?" Leia asked, scanning the hangar.

Just then, they all heard the sound of rolling wheels. Forbee-X, a science research droid, took in the group with her visual sensors. A wide screen took up most of the space in her egg-shaped head. It flashed several different colors before settling on a bright, cheerful blue.

"Greetings, humans and droids," she told them.

"I am ready to board. Leaving is always so stimulating!" Her blue screen flashed so brightly that Threepio was certain his visual sensors would blow.

"I don't agree at all," Threepio protested. "I find leaving terribly distressing. Who knows what perils we will be exposed to on this mission?"

"Look on the bright side." Forbee-X's screen flashed again. "Risks equal opportunity. Experiments! Analysis! Conclusions! Fun!"

"Yes, it must be thrilling for you," Threepio said politely. Now he was especially glad that this would be a short mission. Forbee-X seemed nice enough, but too much enthusiasm made his nerve sensors twitch.

"I saw Zissu talking with Commander Willard," Solo reported. "He should be here soon."

"And Stuart?" Leia asked, turning to Threepio. "You were supposed to keep an eye on him, Threepio."

"I know, Princess Leia," Threepio fretted. "But he always manages to slip away from me. The last time I found him playing space poker with the X-wing pilots."

"How'd he do?" Luke asked, amused.

"He cleaned them out, I'm afraid," Threepio said. "They showed a remarkable lack of skill."

"Hey! He got lucky," Solo protested.

Leia's glance turned frosty. "You were playing

space poker with Governor Zissu's twelve-year-old son?" she asked.

"Listen, sister," Solo said, "that kid is twelve going on thirty. He doesn't need protection from *me*. Did you know he dumped a whole box of Bassel sea salt into the chow yesterday?"

Luke nodded. "I've never seen pilots drink up their weekly ration of water so fast!"

Everyone quieted down when Trux Zissu entered the hangar. Although his hair was silver, he was muscular and fit. He looked more like a fighter than a governor as he strode up to the other Rebels.

"I'm ready to board," he told them.

"I'm afraid the *Timespan* is the only ship we can spare, Governor Zissu," Leia reported. "She's old, but she's spaceworthy."

"I checked her over myself," Han told him. "And just in case of trouble, we tweaked your escape pod to maximum performance."

"Trouble?" Threepio asked.

"I am grateful for all your assistance," Trux Zissu offered warmly. "Are the droids ready, Princess Leia?"

"Excuse me, Captain Solo," Threepio interrupted politely. "When you say *trouble*, do you have something specific in mind?"

But Threepio was drowned out by Leia, who

spoke to Governor Zissu. "Everything is ready. We just can't seem to locate your son."

Trux Zissu grimaced. "Stuart never manages to be on time. But if you look for trouble, my son will be somewhere nearby."

"Speaking of *trouble*," Threepio interjected, "I —"

But Threepio was interrupted by a shout from the direction of the *Timespan*.

"Aha!" Leia said. "It looks like you've found him."

The group hurried over to the transport ship. Rennie Gallou, a supply officer, was firmly gripping Stuart's collar while the slender dark-haired boy tried to wriggle away.

"I found him trying to steal a few pieces of azurite," Rennie reported. She opened her palm. A sizable chunk of the blue mineral winked in the hangar floodlights.

"I thought we might need it to trade with," Stuart told his father. His wide green eyes were tilted at the corners, giving him a mischievous look. He blinked innocently, but no one was fooled. "I was just borrowing them."

"Just in case you find some poker players on Delantine?" Trux Zissu asked sternly.

"Sorry, Father," Stuart muttered.

They all headed toward the *Timespan*. Governor

Zissu walked ahead with Princess Leia. Threepio was right behind them, and heard part of their quiet conversation.

"I'm afraid Stuart has been a handful since his mother died," Zissu told the princess. "I apologize for any trouble he may have caused."

"It's all right, Trux," Leia said. "Look around you. Many of us here were mischievous children once ourselves. And that includes me. Perhaps troublemakers make the best Rebels."

Zissu smiled. "Thank you, Princess Leia. I'll remember that in the future. Well, we'd better get aboard, before Stuart 'borrows' an X-wing."

Everyone stopped at the ramp for the last good-byes. Leia embraced Trux.

"I wish you a safe journey," she said. "May the Force be with you."

"And with you," Trux replied steadily. "I won't fail you, Princess Leia."

Luke Skywalker and Han Solo both shook Trux's hand, and said a short good-bye to Threepio, Artoo, and Forbee-X. No one wanted to linger. Every Rebel knew that any good-bye could be forever.

The droids boarded first. Threepio settled himself into a seat next to Artoo. Forbee-X situated herself behind them. Governor Zissu took his place at the controls, and Stuart sat in the copilot's seat. Soon enough, the blast of the ion rockets filled the air, and the ship trembled as it rose and glided from the hangar. Within seconds, the surface of the Yavin moon became a blur of green and blue as the ship headed toward the upper atmosphere.

They were off!

HYPERSPACE

As soon as Governor Zissu made the jump into hyperspace, everyone began to move around the cabin. Artoo jacked into the navicomputer to monitor the ship's progress. Forbee-X glided over to double-check the equipment she used to collect specimens. She would be doing research for the Rebels on Delantine, which was rich in minerals that could be used in the battle against the Empire.

Threepio stared out the spaceport, wondering about all the star systems they were rushing past. Most of them were probably filled with Imperials. He was glad to be passing them by.

Stuart slid into a seat next to Threepio. "That Forbee-X is hypergalactic," he remarked. "She's the latest in astrodroid design. Did you know she's adaptable to any terrain? She can retract those wheels and use feet if she wants to. Now *that's* a droid!"

"I'm sure she will be helpful to your father on Delantine," Threepio agreed.

"She must make you feel pretty useless," Stuart continued.

Threepio's head swiveled toward Stuart. "Excuse me?"

"She's this fully loaded droid, and what are your programmed skills?" Stuart asked with a shrug. "Making a cup of ti'il tea?"

"I beg your pardon?" Threepio asked frostily.

"Aw, c'mon," Stuart said. "You know you're already an outdated droid."

Threepio reared back. "Outdated? I speak *six million* languages, for your information, and —"

"Wow," Stuart interrupted. "You can make tea in *six million* languages?"

Threepio was afraid his circuits would explode. But luckily, Artoo interrupted with a series of chirps and whistles.

"Oh," Threepio said. "You're teasing me, Master Stuart."

Stuart grinned. "Space travel can get awfully boring," he said. "I like to spice things up. No offense, right?"

"No offense," Threepio said grudgingly.

Stuart wandered off to explore the ship. Artoo chirped at Threepio. "No, Artoo," Threepio said firmly. "It was *not* funny."

Artoo chirped again.

"Not in the least!" Threepio sputtered.

The journey to Delantine went quickly. Artoo spent his time jacked into the ship's library, learning all he could about the Delantine system. Trux Zissu tried to educate himself as well. Forbee-X prepared her lab kit to test minerals. Threepio didn't have much to do, and he certainly wasn't about to make tea for Stuart!

"I know I promised Princess Leia that I would watch over Stuart," Threepio told Artoo. "I don't take that lightly. But it isn't as though she *ordered* me. It was a request. Exactly how far does my responsibility go? I can't watch him every minute."

Forbee could not help but interrupt. "You did not ask my advice, Threepio, but you must understand that Stuart is a young human life-form. Misbehavior is a normal function. Patience is required, and frustration only interferes with your duties. Besides, we are not programmed for it."

"I know," Threepio fretted. "But why do I *feel* it? There is something beyond circuits and connectors, Forbee."

"That is illogical," Forbee-X said, her screen turning murky green. "If you're not programmed for feelings, you shouldn't feel them."

Forbee-X glided away. Artoo gave a low whistle.

"Yes, Artoo," Threepio whispered. "Our latest astrodroid model may have an advanced data system, but she has rather a lot to learn."

"We're coming out of hyperspace," Governor Zissu called.

Stuart slid into the copilot's seat, and everyone else took up secure positions on the bridge.

The ship shuddered as it slowed. The stars seemed to tremble as the *Timespan* rushed toward them. Then the ship eased into realspace, and Zissu checked its coordinates.

"Perfect," he said. "It won't be long now." Suddenly, he leaned forward, straining at the monitor. "There's trouble approaching. An Imperial warship."

"Do you think they're looking for us?" Threepio asked nervously.

"Our departure was top secret," Trux Zissu answered. "Let's just cruise at normal speed. Maybe they'll go by."

Just then, the ship shuddered and pitched violently to the right.

"Hang on!" Zissu cried. "That was a blast from a quad laser cannon. We're under attack!"

SHOWDOWN

Everyone staggered as the laser cannons of the Imperial warship blasted another stunning blow to the *Timespan*.

"Can't you activate the deflector shields?" Threepio asked nervously, hanging onto the console.

"Thanks to that last shot, they're no longer operational," Governor Zissu said tersely. "And I don't think this ship has a chance of outrunning an Imperial warship. The question is, why didn't they broadcast that they wanted to board us? They fired before even sending a signal! They must know I'm aboard." Zissu looked grim. "I fear we've been betrayed."

Another explosion shook the ship. Stuart glanced at the monitor. "They're docking, Dad!" he cried. "They just blasted out the boarding lock!"

Zissu looked over at the droids and his son.

"Everyone to the escape pod. *Now.* I'll hold them off." He tossed a blaster to Stuart. Then he hesitated. He drew Stuart against his chest for a brief moment. "May the Force be with you, my son."

Stuart raised his head. He locked eyes with his father. "I'm not leaving you, Father."

Governor Zissu shook his head. "You must."

They heard the sound of running footsteps. "The stormtroopers are aboard," Governor Zissu said. "It's our only chance to get word back to Princess Leia. Listen to me, Artoo — follow the coordinates already entered in the pod. Now go!"

"You must come now, Master Stuart!" Threepio urged.

Threepio herded Stuart and Forbee-X toward the passageway to the escape pod. Artoo was close behind.

Stuart turned before stepping into the passageway. The stormtroopers had entered the bridge. Stuart watched as his father blasted two to the ground. The next stormtrooper fired, but Zissu leaped onto the console and escaped the blast.

The stormtrooper leveled his blaster. "We have orders to capture or kill, Governor Zissu. Your choice."

Zissu's eyes flicked toward the passageway. His steely gaze told Stuart to *go.*

The governor threw down his blaster. "I don't recognize your authority, but I'll obey."

"Father!" Stuart whispered, starting toward him.

Threepio yanked Stuart backward. He pulled him toward the escape hatch. "We have no time to lose!" he warned.

Artoo activated the hatch. Stuart and the droids sprang into the escape pod. It was crowded, but they all crammed inside. The hatch doors closed behind them.

"Okay, we're here," Stuart said. "Now, who's going to fly this thing?"

"Artoo can," Threepio said. "He piloted us to Tatooine once before in a pod."

Artoo beeped at Threepio.

"Yes, yes, all right," Threepio said. "I'll activate the ship doors while you jack into the navicomputer. Just hurry!"

Stuart sat on the padded gee-couch. He looked dazed.

Suddenly they heard pounding on the hatch. A blow from a laser made the whole pod shudder. Forbee-X's screen turned an alarming red. "May I make a suggestion?" Her calm tone changed to an urgent screech. *"Launch!"*

"Good idea." Threepio listened to Artoo's beeped instructions. He drew the launch lever back, and the escape doors of the *Timespan* opened. Artoo beeped at the navicomputer, which responded with a firing of thrusters. A split second later, the escape pod hurtled out into the stars.

Threepio hurried to stand next to Forbee at the dorsal viewport. They looked back at the Imperial warship.

"They aren't turning," Threepio noted with relief. "They're letting us go. All they wanted was Governor Zissu. We're safe."

Artoo beeped and flashed his red lights.

"Yes, Artoo, I know," Threepio agreed. "Safe for the moment, I should say. The question is, where do we go now?"

DECISIONS

"Father said that coordinates have been entered," Stuart said, rising from the couch. "That means we're heading to Delantine. Lucky we're so close. This sure is a bucket of bolts," he observed, examining the cabin. "How *old* is this thing? It looks like it'll bust apart if we bump against some space dust."

"Master Stuart, it would help if you did not question whether our craft is spaceworthy, considering we're escaping in it," Threepio pointed out. "Besides, Captain Solo and Chewbacca worked on it personally."

Artoo was jacked into the pod's navicomputer. He chirped and rotated his head.

"Really? Oh my," Threepio said. "That's odd."

"Threepio, what is it?" Stuart asked impatiently.

"Artoo says that there were no coordinates entered at all," Threepio said. "Your father was mistaken."

"Father is never mistaken," Stuart said.

"Excuse me for interrupting," Forbee-X said. "But it seems to me that we're on our way to nowhere. Perhaps we should discuss a destination."

"Quite right, Forbee," Threepio said. "What do you think, Artoo?"

"Delantine, of course," Stuart said.

"Excuse me, Master Stuart," Threepio spoke politely, "but I was talking to Artoo. We are *not* going to Delantine. Right, Artoo?"

Before Artoo could answer, Stuart spoke up. "But we're so close to Delantine," he said. "It's the logical choice."

"Delantine is most likely under Imperial control," Threepio argued. "If we land, we'll most certainly be captured, too."

Artoo beeped.

"You see — Artoo agrees with me!" Threepio exclaimed. "We should locate a nearby planet so that we can find a way back to Yavin 4."

Artoo whistled and chirped.

"Exactly, Artoo," Threepio said, nodding. "We have to tell the princess what has occurred. Someone must have known that we were escorting your father on the *Timespan,* Stuart."

"And what about Father?" Stuart argued. "We can't just abandon him. Going back to the base would be a waste of time. He could be on Delantine right now!"

"I'm afraid, Master Stuart, that you are under our charge," Threepio told him. "I told Princess Leia we would watch over you. You must see that we know best."

Stuart took a step toward Threepio. "Listen to me, you heap of metal," he said. "I'm under nobody's charge, get it?"

"There's no need to be nasty," Threepio answered calmly, because even he could see that Stuart was speaking with fear as much as anger. He could not blame the boy for wanting to save his father. "And you *are* under our charge, I'm afraid," Threepio added.

"Am not!"

"Are too!" Threepio snapped.

Artoo gave a series of chirps.

"I said 'are too,' not 'Artoo.' I wasn't calling you," Threepio told the other droid. "Oh, this is all too confusing! I wish Master Luke were here!"

Forbee-X's screen suddenly flashed a series of colors before settling on a cool blue-gray tone. "Let's try to calm down, shall we?" she suggested. "Threepio, you don't *know* that Delantine is under Imperial control. Why don't we activate the comm transceiver and see? Wouldn't that be logical?"

Artoo clicked and whirred.

"Oh, dear," Threepio said. "I'm afraid Artoo already tried to do so. The comm transceiver is inactive. Maybe it got hit by a stray blast from the Imperial warship."

"Then we'll just have to take a chance," Stuart said. "Let's enter the coordinates for Delantine."

"But don't you see that the Imperials could be waiting for us?" Threepio cried, waving his arms in exasperation. "We can't take that chance. There are several planets and moons in the Delantine system that we could land on instead. The sooner we can send a message, the sooner a rescue mission can be launched."

"Rescue mission?" Stuart asked. "Do you think the Rebels will launch one?"

Artoo whistled indignantly.

"As Artoo has pointed out, of course they would. The princess and her friends always protect their own," Threepio said. "Now, we are all in agreement. Artoo, you have to plot a course. This pod isn't carrying much fuel, I am sure."

Artoo beeped several times and rotated his dome-shaped head.

"Artoo thinks that the planet Romm will do," Threepio explained to Stuart. "It has a fairly active port where we could catch a transport. And it's rumored that there's a Rebel faction in the remote hills.

We could try to contact them, if we need to. Although that sounds a bit dangerous to me. Do we agree?"

"Perfectly logical," Forbee-X approved.

"I guess it's okay," Stuart replied.

"All right, then," Threepio said, relieved. "Artoo, you enter the coordinates, and I'll activate the automatic thrusters. Wherever they are," Threepio muttered under his breath. He didn't want Stuart to know that he actually had no idea how to pilot an escape pod. Luckily, most of the piloting controls were automatic.

Threepio squeezed past Stuart to the pilot console. He felt immediately confused. He didn't recognize any of the controls. Then he saw *automated thruster control.*

"Ah, there we are!" he said. "Ready, Artoo?" After an affirmative beep, Threepio pushed the control button. "Oh, dear. Nothing happened, Artoo."

Artoo gave a long series of chirps.

"What did he say?" Stuart asked.

"It seems that the automated controls are broken or locked out," Threepio reported. "How odd."

"Perhaps whoever warned the Imperials about us also tampered with the pod," Stuart spoke up. "Maybe even our comm transceiver."

"Let's not jump to conclusions, Stuart!" Forbee-X said. "Equipment could have been damaged during the Imperial attack."

"All I know is, we have to land *somewhere,*" Threepio said. "Artoo said we can use the emergency manual controls."

Lights flashed on the console in front of Threepio, confusing him. But he didn't want to ask Artoo for help again. Not in front of Stuart.

"Are you sure you know what you're doing?" Stuart asked doubtfully. "Let me take over."

"I can do it!" Threepio said, a little more sharply than he meant to. It was too embarrassing to be ordered around by a young boy.

"Why do you have to fire the thrusters?" Stuart asked. "Artoo already entered our course into the computer. You don't know why, do you?"

"Of course I do," Threepio answered. He wished Forbee-X would interrupt with an explanation, because he actually wasn't sure himself. "If we don't do anything, we'll just keep going in a straight line."

"See-Threepio is not being very scientific," Forbee piped up. "But he is correct, in a crude fashion. The First Law of Motion states that a body in motion — like this ship — will remain in motion *unless* a force acts upon it."

"Say that again?" Stuart said, frowning.

"Why don't I show you what I mean?" Forbee-X asked. Her screen cleared, then filled with a diagram.

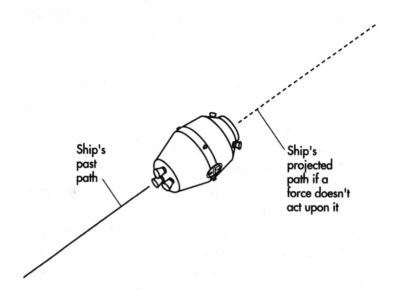

Ship's
past
path

Ship's
projected
path if a
force doesn't
act upon it

"Unless the Force acts upon it?" Threepio asked. "If only Master Luke were with us now — none of us can harness the Force."

"Pipe down, Threepio, I'm trying to get this," Stuart told Threepio impatiently. "Forbee, when you said 'force,' you meant a push or a pull, right?"

"Exactly," Forbee answered. "In our case, force can come from the ship's thrusters —"

"So I was right!" Threepio said triumphantly.

"Lucky guess," Stuart muttered.

"— or a blast from a laser cannon —"

"Thank you, but I'd prefer a different force," Threepio said, wincing.

"— or a comet," Forbee-X said. "Or —"

In order to stop Forbee-X from listing every possible force in the universe, Threepio yanked on the thruster lever.

But instead of rocketing forward, the pod spun to one side and kept turning.

"Whoaaaaa!" Threepio shouted as his head bumped the ceiling. Stuart grabbed the copilot's seat, and his legs rose over his head. Artoo did a somersault and banged against the ceiling. Forbee-X was able to extend her arms to grab the handles on the pod walls.

"Do something, Threepio!" Stuart yelled. "You got us into this!"

"That's not very helpful, you know," Threepio said from the ceiling, where he'd grabbed onto a convenient handle. "I'm doing my very best. Oh, dear. I don't understand what happened at all."

While the pod spun, it also kept moving forward.

"We are out of control," Forbee-X noted.

"Thank you for bringing it to our attention," Threepio said. "Now, can you explain *why?*"

"Absolutely!" Forbee-X responded cheerfully. "That's why I'm here."

A diagram appeared on Forbee's screen. Threepio tilted his head upside down to read it.

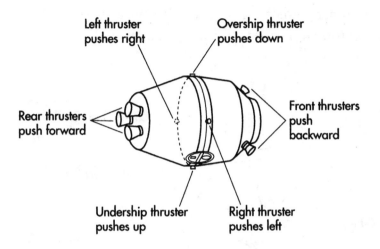

DIRECTIONAL THRUSTERS

Left thruster pushes right

Overship thruster pushes down

Rear thrusters push forward

Front thrusters push backward

Undership thruster pushes up

Right thruster pushes left

"That should make things clear," Forbee said, satisfied.

"Make *what* clear?" Threepio asked. "I can't make head nor tail of it. Maybe it's because I'm upside down."

"Used correctly," Forbee explained, "these thrusters could help us navigate."

"What thrusters did Threepio hit, then?" Stuart asked curiously.

"Good question, Stuart. Let me do a quick calculation." A series of numbers suddenly streamed across Forbee-X's blue screen. "Whew," she said with a happy sigh. "I just love calculating! Anyway, my numbers indicate that Threepio pushed some of the rotational thrusters. I'd say these. Watch!"

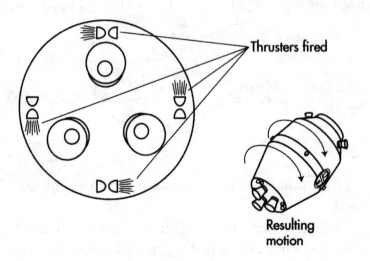

ROTATIONAL THRUSTERS

Thrusters fired

Resulting
motion

"But he's not firing them anymore," Stuart pointed out. "Why are we still spinning?"

"Yes, it would be rather nice to stop," Threepio said. Artoo beeped in agreement.

"Oh. I guess I forgot to mention a new application of the First Law of Motion," Forbee answered. "A body that is spinning keeps spinning unless a force acts on it. In this case, the force could be the opposite thrusters, or, say, if another ship fired on us —"

"Forbee!" Threepio exclaimed, interrupting her. "Can't you think of a less *explosive* example?"

"Okay," Forbee-X agreed. "It could be one of the asteroids in that field ahead."

"Well, that's better than an explosion," Threepio said comfortingly. Then his head swiveled back to Forbee-X. "What did you say?"

"Asteroid field dead ahead," Forbee repeated calmly. "Unless we can change course, we'll run straight into it."

DEAD AHEAD

"Asteroid field?" Threepio cried. Artoo beeped in alarm.

"I suggest we plot a course to escape," Forbee-X advised.

"Now there's an idea," Threepio said.

"Navigation through an asteroid field would be extremely hazardous," Forbee-X continued. "I calculate our odds at —"

"Please don't!" Stuart and Threepio said together.

"I've had enough bad news for one day," Stuart added.

Threepio looked out the viewport. Empty space rushed at him dizzily. Stars cartwheeled by them as they spun through the universe.

But he didn't have to glimpse the asteroid field

to be concerned. And he didn't need Forbee-X to calculate the odds. Asteroids — some the size of small moons — rushed by at amazing speeds. Any one of them would be capable of smashing the tiny escape pod to bits.

"We're doomed!" he cried.

Artoo beeped and chirped.

"I *am* looking on the bright side," Threepio moaned. "At least it will be quick. One smash and we're done for!"

"Aren't there any guts inside that golden shell?" Stuart asked. "C'mon, Threepio. Don't give up on us yet."

Artoo beeped and his head rotated quickly.

"Quite right, Artoo," Threepio said. "This is no time for bickering. If you check the navicomputer, I'll try to get to the console to fire the counter-thrusters."

But try as he might, Threepio could not push himself off the side of the pod. Artoo had similar trouble. Every time one of the droids was able to push off, the motion of the pod would send them flying back against the wall. Threepio yelled to Artoo that he couldn't get to the controls. He also told Artoo he remembered every detail of how they had gotten into this mess. . . .

Artoo's red warning lights began to flicker.

"Oh, Artoo! Keep trying! Forbee, what's going on?" Threepio moaned.

Stuart tried to get to the console, but he could only wiggle his fingers. "Why do my arms feel so heavy?" he asked.

"Artificial gravity is being created by centrifugal force," Forbee-X answered. "That is a force caused by a spinning object, like this pod. It pushes things — like droids or humans — outward. Too much centrifugal force is like too much gravity."

"Is that why my internal sensors say that I've just doubled my weight?" Threepio asked.

Stuart shook his head. "I don't get it. Gravity is what keeps my feet on the ground and causes objects to fall when you drop them. But there's no gravity in space. Right, Forbee?"

"You are almost right, Stuart," Forbee-X replied. "There is very little natural gravity in outer space. But there can be artificial gravity."

"Sure, like the artificial gravity on a space cruiser," Stuart said. "But it never plastered us against the walls like this."

"And it didn't hurt my circuits like this, either," Threepio said. "But how can we fight it? We have to get to the controls!"

"Let's get a clear picture of what's going on," Forbee-X said crisply as her screen flashed.

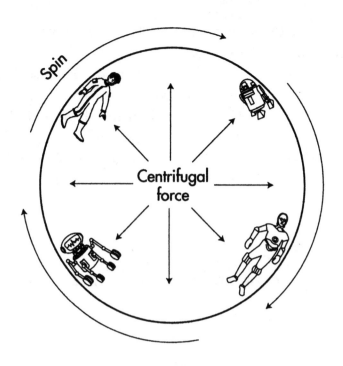

"When Threepio hit the thrusters," Forbee-X explained, "the sudden movement jostled us a bit. Normally, the ship's artificial gravity would have pulled us back down. But the thrusters made the ship spin. The spinning produced the centrifugal force you can see on my screen. The spinning was fast, so the centrifugal force was strong — strong enough to override the ship's artificial gravity. In a sense, we each 'fell' in a different direction."

"Is it the strong centrifugal force that makes us feel so heavy?" Stuart asked.

"Exactly!" Forbee-X exclaimed. Her screen cleared and beamed a sunny yellow before shifting back to blue again. "Strong centrifugal force is like strong gravity. It makes objects — including bodies — feel very, very heavy. Let's take another look. Stuart, may I borrow your image for a moment?"

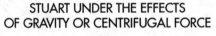

STUART UNDER THE EFFECTS OF GRAVITY OR CENTRIFUGAL FORCE

Low

Stuart's muscles can easily push back against the low gravity or centrifugal force. Without much effort, Stuart can jump really high.

Normal

Stuart's muscles are adapted to this much gravity or centrifugal force. His jump is impressive for a boy of his age, but not spectacular.

High

Stuart's muscles are no match for strong gravity or centrifugal force. Even with a lot of effort, he can hardly lift himself from the ground. You no doubt recognize this as our present situation.

"There!" Forbee-X said, satisfied. "Now everything is clear."

"Crystal clear," Threepio said. "But I *still* can't get to the controls!"

"This feeling reminds me of when I was little," Stuart said. "My dad would grab my arms and swing me around."

"Excellent example!" Forbee-X approved. "That was centrifugal force, too."

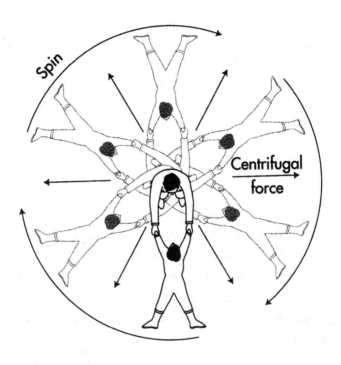

"The faster he swung me around, the more force I felt," Stuart said.

"Exactly!" Forbee's screen flashed several times in

approval before returning to the diagram. "You are an excellent student, Stuart."

"I wish that Father could hear that," Stuart said wistfully. Sadness dimmed his bright green eyes.

"He will, one day very soon," Forbee-X said softly.

"So what should we *do*?" Threepio asked.

"I'm afraid I can't help much there," Forbee said, her screen turning deep blue. "You're just going to have to push as hard as you can. Maybe you can fight the centrifugal force."

Threepio struggled against what felt like a ton of heavy blankets weighing him down. "I can't!"

"Hmmmm. Would it help if you knew that it's our only hope?" Forbee asked. Her screen was growing red. "The asteroid field is approaching rapidly."

"That helps, most definitely," Threepio responded. He threw himself against the force and managed to grab the next handle on the pod. He pulled himself a few inches forward.

Stuart managed to hook a foot around the edge of the padded gee-couch. Using that as leverage, he grabbed the edge of the cushion and yanked himself forward.

"Good work, Master Stuart!" Threepio said. "Now, if we can just get to the console. . . ."

Artoo beeped frantically. He couldn't dislodge himself from the wall.

"I'll get you in a minute, Artoo," Threepio called. "At least, I hope so." As the pod spun, he grabbed onto the edge of a storage rack. His head banged against the wall as he pulled himself closer to the console. "Oh dear. This is worse than a gravel storm on Tatooine. I hope I'm not dented," Threepio moaned.

"I have bruises on top of my bruises," Stuart grunted. "The important thing is to get to the console, golden boy. If you reach the pilot's seat, I'll buff you until you shine like a supernova."

"I'll . . . take . . . you . . . up on that!" Threepio said as he hauled himself along the pod floor. But as the pod revolved, the floor became the ceiling. Then it became the floor again. "Lucky I'm not human," Threepio added. "I'd be terribly dizzy right now."

"Well, I *am* human," Stuart gasped. "And you're right."

Finally, Threepio made it underneath the controls. He clung to the pole that anchored the pilot's chair to the floor. Stuart hung on to the copilot's chair.

"All right, we're here at last," Threepio said. "What should I do?"

"Wait, I have a suggestion," Stuart said. "Why don't you do the *opposite* of what you did before?"

"Really, Master Stuart. Does being testy make things any better?" Threepio scolded.

"But he's right!" Forbee-X announced. "Threepio

used the thrusters to apply forces in certain directions —"

"I've got it!" Stuart crowed, interrupting. "So we
should use the thrusters to apply forces in the opposite directions!"

"I was going to say that!" Threepio protested.

Stuart and Threepio both dove for the controls at
the same time. They knocked heads with a *crack*.

"Ow!" Stuart cried, rubbing his forehead. "Now
I'm *really* dizzy!"

"Sorry, Master Stuart. Am I dented?" Threepio
fretted.

"Ha! Another illustration of theory," Forbee-X
announced. "Stuart, you went toward the controls
with a certain force. Threepio met you with an equal
amount of force. Now both of your bodies are at rest!"

Artoo beeped insistently.

"Yes, Artoo, the asteroid field," Threepio said
hurriedly as he reached for the controls. "Just let
me —"

But he didn't get a chance to finish. Stuart reached
for the thruster control at the same time, and they col-
lided again. This time, Threepio accidentally pushed a
lever forward with his elbow.

"Oh, no, that's another set of rotational thrus —"
Stuart started, but he didn't get a chance to finish.
With a lurch, the pod suddenly began to career
wildly. This time, the tumbling was even worse. The

pod tossed and turned as if it were a small rock being shaken by a ferocious rancor.

As Threepio tumbled, Stuart got tangled in his legs. The two of them fell backward, then slammed against the ceiling of the pod. Artoo bounced from one wall to another. Forbee-X curled her long fingers and toes around safety handles. One of the storage compartments opened, and medpacks and glow rods suddenly flew through the cabin. One of the rods hit Threepio in the head.

"Hold on!" Forbee-X cried.

"To *what*?" Threepio yelled as he slammed against the floor again. He grabbed a corner of the gee-couch. Stuart grabbed another corner just as a second compartment sprang open. Survival food packets and gear rained down on their heads.

But Threepio hardly noticed. He watched in horror as Artoo bounced from the ceiling to the floor and back again. Without long arms and legs, Artoo could not grab onto any handles or furniture. As he tumbled end over end, Artoo slammed against the walls, floor, and ceiling. His warning lights flickered.

"Artoo!" Threepio cried.

Artoo gave a faint beep. Then he slammed against the wall again. The door to an emergency storage unit sprang open and crashed on top of his dome-shaped head. His lights flickered, then went out.

"Artoo!" Threepio cried. "Artoo!"

ONE WILD RIDE

"We've got to stabilize this ship," Forbee-X urged.

"No kidding," Stuart grunted as a particularly hard jolt sent his head crashing against a chair. "This is one wild ride!"

"Threepio fired a new combination of rotational thrusters," Forbee-X told them. Her screen flashed.

We were spinning around just one axis.

Now we are spinning around two.

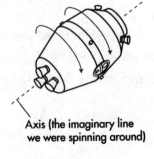

Axis (the imaginary line we were spinning around)

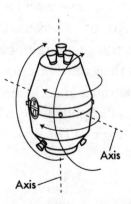

Axis

Axis

"That is why the ride is so bumpy," Forbee explained.

Threepio crawled toward Artoo. He joggled the smaller droid's emergency switch. "Artoo, you mustn't leave me now!" he cried. "Wake up!"

But all of Artoo's sensors had shut down. The last blow had been too much for him.

Stuart wedged himself against the controls by tying his belt around the pilot's seat. "Okay, Forbee," he called, "I'm here. Give me a crash course in space piloting."

"Oh, dear," Threepio moaned. "Did you have to say *crash*?"

"I'm not coded for pilot lessons," Forbee-X answered. "Is the R2 unit operational? We need his skills to navigate and plot a course."

"I can't revive him, I'm afraid," Threepio said. "He's shut down. Oh, Artoo!"

"Threepio, you've got to fix him," Forbee-X said worriedly. "I have scientific principles for flight encoded in my data bank, but no practical knowledge."

"And we're still out of control!" Stuart pointed out as the pod bumped and zigzagged. Threepio was slammed against the side of the pod again.

"Just tell him the principles, and we'll figure out the application," Threepio suggested.

"It's worth a try," Forbee-X agreed. Her screen brightened into a determined blue. "I will report what's stored in my data banks. First I have to calculate the precise amount of force needed and the direction in which to apply it." Forbee-X's viewscreen suddenly filled with more numbers and symbols. "This is my favorite part," she told them as her screen glowed.

"Do hurry!" Threepio called as he bent over Artoo again. "I can't do anything if the ship keeps turning like this!"

"First, we must straighten out our flight path," Forbee-X said. "Otherwise, Stuart won't be able to steer through the asteroid field. Can you find the opposite rotational thrusters, Stuart?"

"Got them," Stuart answered. "But which ones should I push?"

"I don't know," Forbee-X said worriedly. "I don't know which ones were pushed in the first place."

"Oh dear," Threepio moaned.

"Wait!" Stuart called. "Here's a lever for an emergency stabilizer. Should I try it?"

"What do we have to lose?" Threepio asked.

"Okay, everyone. Hang on!" Stuart drew back the lever. A burst of speed sent them one way, then the other. Then, in a series of tiny movements, the pod shuddered and corrected itself. They were flying straight again!

"Whew, that was close," Stuart said. "What now?"

"The first principle of space flight is that thrusters

are used to apply force in an opposite direction," Forbee-X instructed.

Stuart nodded. "I get it. So if I fire the left thruster, we'll go right."

"Right," Forbee agreed.

"No, I said left," Stuart said.

"Right," Forbee answered.

"Oh, heavens! Say 'affirmative,' Forbee, you're confusing Master Stuart!" Threepio cried. "Not to mention *me*."

"Oh, sorry!" Forbee said cheerfully. "Affirmative, Stuart. Left thruster, go right."

"Okay, everyone — brace yourselves!" Stuart called.

He pushed at the left thruster lever. The pod swayed a hair to the right.

"Excellent!" Threepio announced dryly. "Now we'll probably hit the first asteroid just a little to the right, instead of dead-on."

Stuart made a face at Threepio. "What happened?" he asked Forbee-X. "I thought that the left thruster would push us to the right."

"We *are* moving to the right," Forbee-X explained. "But we're also moving forward."

Stuart frowned. "Does that mean I have to push against the push? If I fire the forward thruster, the backward force will slow us down. Especially if I add plenty of power."

"Actually —" Forbee-X began to say. At that moment, Stuart fired the thruster. The droids pitched forward violently, and Stuart hit his head on the console.

"Master Stuart? We seem to be going *backward*," Threepio said. "Maybe you should do the *opposite* of what you just did."

"You just applied a bit too much thrust, that's all," Forbee-X said encouragingly. "Try again."

"Thanks for the advice," Stuart said, rubbing his head. "Okay. I'll fire the rear thruster with an equal amount of force. That will get us back to our original direction and speed."

Stuart fired the rear thruster. This time, everyone was pitched backward. Threepio hit his head on the side of the pod again. "Now I *am* dented!" he wailed.

"Sorry about that," Stuart said cheerfully. "But at least we're heading in the right direction. Now I just need a small backward push to slow us down. Add some thrust to the right. Good — now we're making a nice, wide turn. We should miss the asteroid field by a few kilometers. But I guess we should recalculate our course."

"But that's Artoo's job," Threepio said. "And how do you know we've missed the field? We don't know how large it is. But if you can keep the pod steady like this, I might be able to fix Artoo."

"Excellent idea, Threepio," Forbee approved.

"But I don't think we have time. We have to navigate."

"But we have to navigate *somewhere*!" Threepio pointed out, still bent over Artoo. "We need to plot a course."

"No, we don't," Forbee replied, her screen glowing crimson.

"Why not?" Threepio turned around, exasperated. At that moment, a huge asteroid loomed in the viewport, heading straight toward them. Threepio could almost count the molecules of its surface.

"Because we are about to be space dust," Forbee-X pointed out.

CRASH COURSE

For a moment, Stuart and Threepio stood frozen. The gray haze ahead of them was actually a field full of careening asteroids.

"Master Stuart, may I suggest you make a hard left?" Threepio said, his eyes on the asteroid.

"No problem. I've got this baby down," Stuart said confidently. He jerked the thruster control, and the pod lurched to the side. They were about to lose control again!

"Not that hard!" Threepio screamed.

Stuart corrected the maneuver. They came within a bantha whisker of the asteroid.

"Weeeee-hah!" Stuart yodeled. "Did you see that? Hypergalactic!"

"Yes, I did," Threepio said. "Now, would you mind doing it one more time? *Immediately?*"

Another asteroid was bearing down on them. This time, Stuart fired the left thruster. He added forward thrust, and they rocketed past the asteroid, only to be heading toward a bigger one.

Threepio howled and threw his hands over his eyes. He pitched to the left as Stuart fired the thrusters again.

"Yes!" Stuart yelled. "*Now* we're cooking!"

"Master Stuart, do you have to fire the thrusters at full power?" Threepio asked as he crashed against Forbee-X.

"This speed requires sharp, high power turns," Forbee-X offered. "If you slow down, you can plan each turn better and use lower powered, gentler turns. That would give you more control, not to mention that—"

"Whoa! That was a close one!" Stuart shouted. He fired a forward thruster and a backward thruster at the same time. The pod shuddered, then seemed to hang in space for a moment. Stuart hit the left thruster full force, and they swerved to the right. He shouted a yodel that Threepio was sure would short-circuit his auditory sensors.

"Master Stuart, please slow down!" Threepio called, but Stuart was too busy firing thrusters and zooming past asteroids to pay attention. "If I were human, I'd have goose bumps," Threepio added fretfully. "I think I *do* have goose bumps."

"We are almost through the field," Forbee-X announced, her screen flashing nervous orange.

"Thank heavens," Threepio breathed.

He turned his attention back to the viewscreen. He reared back when the largest asteroid of all loomed directly ahead.

"M-master Stuart . . ." Threepio stuttered.

"No problemo, Threepio," Stuart said confidently. His fingers stroked the thruster controls.

"Aren't you going to do something?" Threepio demanded.

"In a minute . . ." Stuart said, concentrating as the asteroid came closer and closer.

"*Anything?*" Threepio wailed.

In a sudden movement, Stuart hit the thruster full power. The pod made a sharp right turn and zoomed past the asteroid.

"We're through!" Stuart exclaimed. "We made it!"

Threepio thumped Artoo. "Did you see that, Artoo? Oh, I suppose not. Well done, Master Stuart!"

Stuart spun around on the chair. His black hair was sticking straight up in front from having his sweaty hands run through it. "Now *that's* space piloting!" he crowed.

"Now, let's not go overboard," Threepio warned. "And I must add that you cut that last maneuver awfully close. I can't help thinking that it was deliberate."

Stuart grinned. "A kid has got to have fun, Threepio. Even trapped in an escape pod with a bunch of droids."

"Fun? You were lucky you didn't get us all killed," Threepio scolded.

"Excuse me for interrupting," Forbee-X said. "But may I point out that we have more important things to do than quarrel? Look ahead."

"Not another asteroid field, I hope," Threepio said, swiveling to peer out the viewport.

A planet rose in the distance. Clouds covered its surface, and Threepio could count three suns in his visual field.

"I wonder what planet it is," Threepio said. "With three suns, it can't be Romm. We're terribly lost. We might even be out of the Delantine system completely."

"It could be an Imperial planet," Stuart said with a shiver. Suddenly, the blood-red clouds looked menacing.

"The cloud cover is extensive," Forbee-X observed. "And something about the orbit of the planet is odd. I haven't seen such a planet in my travels. I need time to compute."

"I suggest we avoid it," Threepio said, still staring at the deep red clouds. "There's no telling what we'd find. If we keep going, we're bound to find a planet we recognize. Now that Stuart knows how to fly, we should have no problem."

"I wouldn't say that," Forbee-X warned.

"Forbee, do you have to be so negative?" Threepio complained. He was hardly ever snappish. After all, he was programmed for politeness. But he didn't like the look of the forbidding, cloudy planet. Being frightened often made him cross.

"I cannot turn a negative into a positive, just because you want me to," Forbee-X said huffily. "It wouldn't be logical."

Oh dear, now I've hurt her feelings, Threepio thought. *Without Artoo, I get myself into all kinds of trouble.*

Stuart spoke up before Threepio could apologize. "What do you mean, Forbee?" he asked.

"We are beginning to feel the planet's gravitational pull," Forbee-X said as numbers and formulas flickered across her viewscreen.

"So?" Stuart asked. "I can just pilot around it."

Forbee-X's screen blinked. "At the risk of sounding *negative*, I must disagree," she said with a glance at Threepio.

Forbee-X's long metal-scaled finger pointed to the console. Threepio followed the direction and saw a flashing red light.

"We can't pilot around the planet. We are about to run out of fuel," Forbee-X announced.

RUNNING ON E

"What next!" Threepio cried. "Artoo, this is all your fault." Looking over at the astromech droid, Threepio remembered that Artoo couldn't hear him, and he felt worse than ever.

"Low fuel?" Stuart asked in disbelief. "But we only went through that tiny asteroid field. How could that be?"

"Let me check the data," Forbee said. Her screen filled with more numbers. She whirred and clicked the way she did when she was truly concentrating. "Oh."

"Oh?" Threepio prompted uneasily.

"Well," Forbee started. She sounded uncomfortable. "Perhaps I should have mentioned that every time Stuart fired the thrusters, it burned extra fuel. The bigger the thrust, the more fuel was burned. A straighter path would have given us a smoother ride, of course. And it would have saved fuel. Our path was more like this."

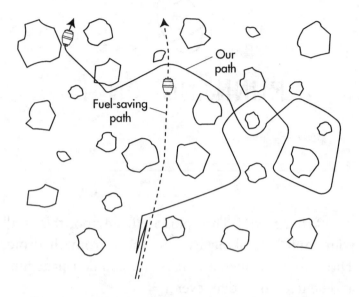

Our path

Fuel-saving path

Threepio waved his arms. "If you'll recall, I did ask you to use less thrust, Master Stuart! Now look what a mess we're in!"

"We can't waste time arguing about it now," Stuart said. "Why don't we just go into orbit around the planet? The inhabitants will probably send a ship up to investigate, and we'd be rescued."

"What if the planet is uninhabited?" Threepio asked. "Or full of Imperials? We could be arrested!"

"Do you have another suggestion?" Stuart asked impatiently. "Because if we run out of fuel, you can imagine what will happen."

"Actually, I *can't*," Threepio admitted. "What *would* happen?" He turned to Forbee-X.

"If we run out of fuel in space, we will keep traveling in a straight line — potentially for millions of years," Forbee-X explained. "We will run out of food for Stuart, of course. And we droids would have no maintenance checks and will eventually have to shut down. Plus, there is the danger of running into an asteroid or planet, since we would have no thruster power to maneuver —"

"Stop, stop!" Threepio cried. He gazed out the viewport at the planet. "Perhaps you're right, Master Stuart. Orbiting would mean going around and around the planet — *not* hurtling off in a straight line to heaven knows where. That sounds like just the thing."

"Would we have enough fuel to stay in orbit, Forbee?" Stuart asked.

"We wouldn't need fuel to *stay* in orbit," Forbee-X responded. "Just like we don't need fuel to keep traveling now, only to fire thrusters to change speed and direction. Don't forget the First Law of Motion. A body in motion stays in the same motion until a force acts on it. But we would need fuel to maneuver ourselves *into* orbit."

"There!" Threepio approved. "So we're agreed. We'll pull up next to the planet and slip into orbit. Simple. Lesson one for a starfighter, I believe."

"Actually," Forbee-X said, "an orbit is a very delicate balance between a planet's gravity and a spacecraft's speed." Forbee-X's screen cleared.

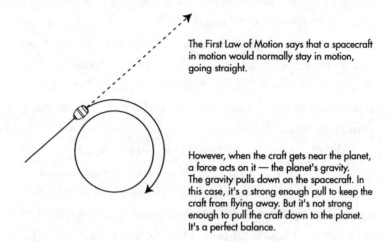

The First Law of Motion says that a spacecraft in motion would normally stay in motion, going straight.

However, when the craft gets near the planet, a force acts on it — the planet's gravity. The gravity pulls down on the spacecraft. In this case, it's a strong enough pull to keep the craft from flying away. But it's not strong enough to pull the craft down to the planet. It's a perfect balance.

"That looks like a cinch," Stuart said confidently.

"When the balance of forces is right, you can do it easily," Forbee-X agreed. "But if the balance is off — even just a little — we will not make it into orbit. It's much more likely that we will miss the planet entirely, as you can see." Her screen flashed.

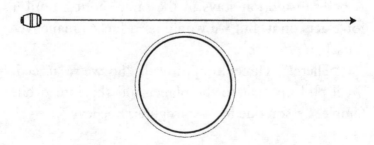

"Or we could be pulled by the gravity, but then escape it and get thrown off on another path."

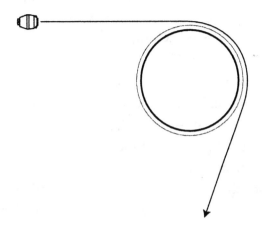

"Or we might even *skip off* the planet's atmosphere like a stone skipping over water."

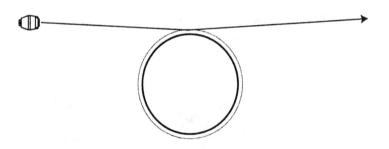

"Or —"

"All this doom and gloom!" Threepio sighed. "Why isn't there a simple solution?"

"Or there is the most likely event in this case," Forbee-X continued.

"We're saved?" Threepio asked hopefully.

"No, we don't have to worry about getting into orbit at all," Forbee-X said.

"Oh, hooray! We *are* saved!" Threepio cried. "Artoo, did you hear that? We're saved!"

"Not quite," Forbee-X said. "In fact, we are being drawn downward — toward the planet."

"What?" Stuart exclaimed. "Do you mean we're going to crash? You'd better explain, Forbee-X."

"And quickly, please," Threepio added, looking nervously out at the planet. It loomed awfully close.

"How about another diagram?" Forbee-X asked brightly. "I think it's called for."

THE FORCE OF GRAVITY

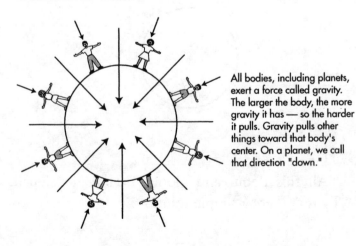

All bodies, including planets, exert a force called gravity. The larger the body, the more gravity it has — so the harder it pulls. Gravity pulls other things toward that body's center. On a planet, we call that direction "down."

"So how can we fight the force of gravity?" Stuart asked. "Wait — I know! I can apply equal force in the opposite direction. A backward thrust!"

Stuart fired the thruster. The pod shuddered as it slowed. They seemed to hang in midair for a moment.

"Oh, dear," Threepio whispered.

Then the pod began to fall again.

"Oh, dear!" Threepio wailed.

"What's happening?" Stuart asked desperately.

"One moment," Forbee-X said crisply. Numbers streamed across her blue screen. "I'm afraid you have burned up the rest of our fuel, Stuart."

Stuart looked pale. "I did?"

"Don't worry — we do have emergency fuel," Forbee-X reassured them. "It's just not available yet. It's loading now. We'll need it to pilot the pod if we reach inner atmosphere."

"Then I wish it would hurry," Threepio said. "We're dropping awfully fast."

"But why didn't the thrust stop us?" Stuart asked.

"It did," Forbee-X answered. "We were stopped for as long as you kept thrusting against the gravity. When the fuel ran out, we lost our upward force."

"And gravity's downward force continued," Stuart finished. "So we're going down."

"Not to add another complication," Threepio put in politely. He was trying to hold onto his manners in the face of disaster. "But it's getting rather hot in here. I hope Artoo doesn't overheat. His circuits have had enough of a bashing for one day."

Stuart wiped at the sweat on his forehead. "It *is* hot. What's going on, Forbee?"

"Let me check some data," Forbee-X said, her circuits clicking. "We are not moving through empty space anymore. We're falling through air. The air is whizzing past us — rubbing the side of the pod as it goes. That rubbing causes friction. Friction creates heat." Forbee-X clicked and whirred. "For example, don't humans rub their hands together to warm them, Stuart?"

"Sure. But doesn't friction slow you down?" Stuart asked. "When I ride my skatecoaster, I brake by rubbing my shoe against the ground."

"Good deduction, Stuart," Forbee-X answered. "And true. Friction with the air is also called *drag*. It's slowing us down right now."

"That's good!" Threepio cried.

"It's just not slowing us down *enough*," Forbee-X continued.

"Oh," Threepio said. "That sounds bad."

"One reason we aren't slowed further is the pod's shape," Forbee-X explained. "It's designed to slip through the air with as little drag as possible. Such a shape is called *aerodynamic*."

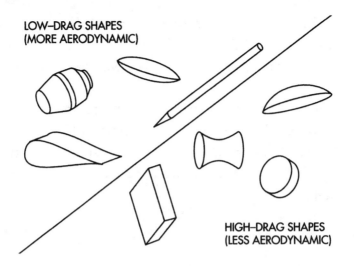

LOW-DRAG SHAPES
(MORE AERODYNAMIC)

HIGH-DRAG SHAPES
(LESS AERODYNAMIC)

"Can you see what I mean?" Forbee-X asked. "We need to add resistance. More *drag,* in other words."

"But how?" Threepio asked.

Forbee-X clicked, and her screen went back to blue. "I'm not sure," she said. "But I suggest we search the pod. Perhaps we could find what we need."

Threepio bent over Artoo. "I'm sorry I said it was your fault. I'm sure you can come up with a solution, Artoo. Wake up!"

"Forget it, Threepio," Stuart said, opening a supply cabinet. "There's no time to tend to Artoo. We have to think. How can we find drag? I wish this pod wasn't so basic."

Threepio's gaze traveled upward from Artoo toward the emergency cabinet. "Wait a moment, Master Stuart. Maybe what we need *is* the basics!"

Stuart looked on curiously as Threepio opened a control panel in the emergency cabinet.

"We have reached inner atmosphere of the planet," Forbee-X announced hurriedly. Her screen flashed.

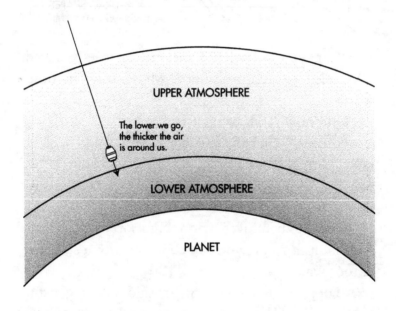

UPPER ATMOSPHERE

The lower we go, the thicker the air is around us.

LOWER ATMOSPHERE

PLANET

"Here it is!" Threepio cried. "A lever for a parachute! It's for emergency use, if the thrusters fail. Hang on!"

Threepio tugged on the lever. It didn't budge. "Oh, no! All that bouncing must have damaged it. Help me, Master Stuart!"

Stuart vaulted over the gee-couch and placed his hands on the lever next to Threepio's. "One, two, three!" he said, yanking down on the lever. It didn't move.

"Let me try," Forbee-X suggested. "We don't have much time." Forbee-X placed her fingers over Stuart's and Threepio's. "One, two, three!" she called.

The three simultaneously yanked on the lever. They pulled so hard that they pulled it out of the socket.

"Oh, no!" Threepio exclaimed. "Now we're truly doomed!"

Suddenly, the pod gave a great lurch upward.

"Wait," Forbee-X said. "We may have broken the lever, but I think we succeeded."

Threepio peered out the viewport. By tilting his head back, he could see the great silver parachute that was now above them, slowing their descent. It glowed red in the atmosphere.

"Look," he said, pointing it out to Stuart. "It's made of spun carbon filaments. It's strong, and it won't catch on fire. There's our resistance!"

"Hypergalactic!" Stuart beamed.

"We're saved! I saved us, Artoo!" Threepio crowed.

"Well, actually . . ." Forbee-X began.

Stuart and Threepio exchanged a frustrated glance. Slowly, they turned to the droid. Formulas flew across Forbee-X's red screen. Finally, the numbers stopped.

"Okay, Forbee," Stuart said. "What's the bad news this time?"

"We are in hypergalactic big trouble," Forbee-X announced.

EMERGENCY LANDING

"Perhaps you'd better explain further," Threepio said.

"The parachute will slow the craft down," Forbee-X explained. "That's good. But the pod must still be piloted to a safe landing. If not, it will crash."

"That's bad," Threepio moaned.

"And we won't have enough fuel for the thrusters, I guess," Stuart said, discouraged.

"Affirmative," Forbee-X agreed. "The emergency fuel has finished loading. But inner atmosphere flight is different from spaceflight. We need wings to pilot safely."

"Wait! I saw a lever for wings in the emergency control box," Threepio said. He scrambled over to the cabinet. "Here!" He pulled back the lever. There was a whirring noise, then a bump.

Stuart peered out the viewport. "Wings! Now we're getting somewhere!"

Numbers flew across Forbee-X's screen. "My calculations show that we're still dropping too fast," she said urgently. "We need to do something. Any ideas?"

"I've got it," Stuart said confidently. "We just need to fire the undership thruster for some upward force."

He pressed the button. There was a flat buzzing sound, and a flashing red light appeared.

"The undership thruster is off-line!" Threepio exclaimed in dismay. "Oh, what else can go wrong?"

"Let me scan my data banks," Forbee-X said, her circuits clicking. "Ah, here's the problem. An inner-atmosphere navigation system doesn't use the undership thruster — or the overship thruster. In fact, it only uses the rear thruster and the small rotational thrusters."

"So we can only go forward or around and around?" Stuart asked in disbelief. "Great. We're the universe's biggest beamdrill!"

"Not exactly, Stuart. This is actually *not* bad news," Forbee-X said cheerfully.

"At last," Threepio breathed.

"According to my data bank, we don't need the other thrusters," Forbee-X continued. "The wings have movable flaps on them. The navigation system uses wing flaps to steer — with a little help from the rotational thrusters. That is the difference between inner- and outer-space navigation."

Stuart slid into the pilot's seat. He put his hands on the controls. "Okay. Before I begin, is there anything else I should know?"

"You control the rear thruster directly," Forbee-X informed him. "That is important because we must keep moving forward. It is the only practical way to keep air rushing by us. And it is that rushing air that is holding us up. Take a look at this diagram before you begin. It might help."

The wing is curved on top. The air sliding over the wing has farther to travel than the air sliding below it. That means that the air above has to travel *faster* than the air below.

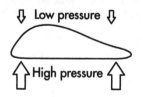

Faster-moving air has less air pressure than slower-moving air. Less air pressure means less pushing power. In a sense, the air beneath the wing overpowers the air above it — pushing the wing up.

"Okay, I've got it," Stuart said. "I think."

"I *hope*," Threepio murmured.

Stuart fired the rear thruster. Immediately, they felt the pod slow. He pushed the joystick, and the pod moved to the right.

"I have control!" he said.

"Excellent," Forbee-X approved. "Now, concentrate on flying, Stuart. But if you need more help, look at this."

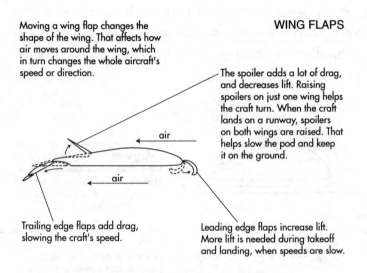

Moving a wing flap changes the shape of the wing. That affects how air moves around the wing, which in turn changes the whole aircraft's speed or direction.

WING FLAPS

The spoiler adds a lot of drag, and decreases lift. Raising spoilers on just one wing helps the craft turn. When the craft lands on a runway, spoilers on both wings are raised. That helps slow the pod and keep it on the ground.

air

air

Trailing edge flaps add drag, slowing the craft's speed.

Leading edge flaps increase lift. More lift is needed during takeoff and landing, when speeds are slow.

Stuart nodded as he stole glances at the diagram. "I understand, Forbee. It's really not that complicated."

"I'm so glad you said that, Master Stuart," Threepio said. "Do you think you can land safely?"

"Sure," Stuart said. But perspiration beaded on

his forehead. His hand gripped the joystick tightly. "I guess."

"Please don't guess," Threepio begged.

Suddenly, an alarm sounded in the cabin. The emergency fuel light flashed. "We do not have much fuel left," Forbee-X warned.

"Forbee, is there anything else on board we could use for fuel?" Stuart asked.

"Hang on. Let me read my data banks. . . ." Forbee-X began clicking and whirring. "The pod's fuel consists of two liquids that explode when mixed. Like this."

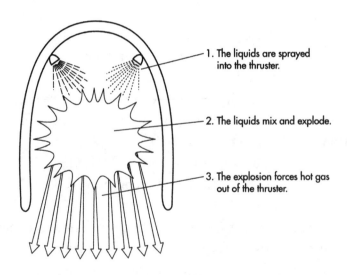

1. The liquids are sprayed into the thruster.

2. The liquids mix and explode.

3. The explosion forces hot gas out of the thruster.

"Unfortunately, we do not have more of those two liquids," Forbee continued.

"A simple 'no' would have done it." Stuart sighed.

"I suggest that we make visual contact with a landing site," Forbee-X said. "And I suggest we do it *fast*."

All three of them peered through the viewport. "We don't want to land in water," Threepio said. "I'm not certain the pod will float, or for how long. And we'll want to refuel and take off again. *If* we can find help."

"Is that a city in the distance?" Stuart asked, squinting. "Where are the macrobinoculars, Threepio?"

"I don't know," Threepio said, looking around the cabin. "All the emergency equipment fell out during your asteroid joyride."

"He doesn't have time to find them," Forbee-X said crisply. "We're losing altitude fast. Not to mention fuel."

"But if there's a city —" Stuart started.

"We should avoid it," Threepio interrupted. "We could be captured!"

"We'll have to explore after we land," Forbee agreed. "Look, Stuart — to your left. After that hill and those trees, there's a flat plain that might do the trick."

"I see it," Stuart said.

"If we follow scientific principles, we should succeed," Forbee-X said. "The main thing is to stay calm."

The hill loomed toward them. "You're coming in too fast!" Threepio shrieked, waving his arms.

"Slow speed," Forbee-X directed.

"You're too low! We're going to hit!" Threepio yelped.

"Hard right," Forbee-X shouted.

The pod skimmed the edge of the hill, barely missing it.

"Don't yell at me!" Stuart exclaimed. He let go of the joystick to wipe sweat from his forehead. The pod skimmed the tops of some trees. They heard a loud *crack* as branches snapped off.

"Please land this thing before we're all killed, Master Stuart," Threepio begged.

With a lurch, the pod dipped. The plain rose before them. The pod seemed to be going entirely too fast, in Threepio's opinion. He was sure they were going to crash.

The engine began to sputter. "I'm losing control!" Stuart yelled.

MAROONED

"Land it!" Forbee-X cried. She had never sounded so emotional before, and her screen was a fiery red. That made Threepio even more panicky. He fell next to Artoo and held onto the storage rack. There was no time to strap himself into a seat.

The pod skimmed just a few feet off the ground. Stuart pushed the joystick, and the pod slammed against the planet's surface. Metal squealed and groaned as the skin of the craft was battered by the surface. It skipped once in the air, then came down harder.

"We're doomed!" Threepio shrieked.

"I can't stop it!" Stuart shouted.

A shower of dirt and rocks hit the pod as it scraped along the surface. It rose in the air again and tilted on its side. From his position, Threepio could see out the viewscreen. They were speeding ahead toward a large boulder.

"Do something, Master Stuart!" Threepio called.

"I don't have control," Stuart said, his eyes on the boulder as the pod bounced down again. Pieces of equipment flew around the cabin, and Forbee was thrown back against the couch.

"Everyone in crash position!" Forbee-X ordered.

A hard bounce almost sent Stuart flying out of the pilot's chair. He gripped the console.

"Here it comes!" he shouted.

With a horrible groaning sound, the pod scraped over pebbles and dirt. But inches away from the boulder, the pod suddenly settled into a patch of soft sand.

Silence settled over them.

"Thank goodness for friction. Is everyone still in one piece?" Forbee-X asked, her screen wavering between gray and red.

"I think so," Threepio said, checking an elbow joint. "A few loose connections, but not too bad, considering that landing."

"Whew," Stuart said. "That was a close one."

"Closer than I'd like," Threepio said fervently.

Stuart grinned shakily. "I hate to admit it, but I'm with you, Threepio." He sprang up and started toward the hatch. "Now let's check out this jerkwater planet."

"Wait!" Forbee-X ordered. "Let me do some

scanning first. I'll interface with the pod's outside environmental sensors."

Stuart grimaced, but he stayed inside the pod. Threepio peered out the viewport nervously. He expected to see Imperial stormtroopers at any moment.

"Ooh, watch out, Threepio," Stuart teased. "Your scaredy-cat sensors look like they're in overdrive."

"Droids have courage," Threepio answered huffily. "But we are also programmed for reasonable caution."

Just then, a weak beep sounded through the cabin.

"Artoo! You're back!" Threepio hurried to his friend. Artoo emitted a series of slow beeps, and one light flashed weakly. But then the beeps got faster, and all his lights began to flash.

"The landing must have knocked your connections back into working order! What luck!" Threepio exclaimed.

Artoo chirped quickly. Threepio told him what had happened.

"This is strange," Forbee-X mused. "Very strange indeed. I am receiving all sorts of contradictory readings. But temperature and air readings support human life, so we can exit the pod."

Stuart pressed the lever for the escape hatch. It

slid open, and the ramp slid downward, extending to the surface.

The droids and Stuart stepped out. "Not much humidity," Threepio noted. "I won't rust, thank goodness."

Everyone gazed around at the strange planet. The soil was dusty, but there was plenty of vegetation. The branches of a nearby grove of trees were full of small green leaves. A blue lake glinted in the distance.

Forbee-X extended her shiny metallic legs and began to explore, lifting one leg gracefully, then the other. Two sensor antennae rose from her oval head. "Strange," she said. "I cannot compute these readings . . . maybe my data bank was damaged in the crash."

"Forbee-X, can we get the pod moving again?" Threepio asked. There was something about the planet that made his sensors tickle. He had a feeling something bad was going to happen. "Can't we just point the pod straight up and use what little bit of fuel we have left to launch ourselves into space? Eventually, we would run across a ship that could refuel us."

Stuart spoke up before Forbee-X could reply. "You'd better fire up those circuits again, Threepio. No way, no how. Gravity brought us down here, remember? In order to escape gravity's downward force, we'd have to fight it with a greater upward force. That would take way more fuel than we have, I'd bet. Right, Forbee-X?"

"You think like a science droid, Stuart," Forbee-X noted approvingly. "That was a very logical conclusion. And absolutely correct."

"So we're stuck here," Threepio said, discouraged.

Artoo clicked and chirped.

"Look on the bright side?" Threepio asked. "I can't imagine what that could be."

"Let's do some exploring," Stuart suggested. "I'll climb that ridge and see if I can spot anything. We need to send a distress signal — and get my father some help!"

"Don't go too far!" Threepio called as Stuart ran off.

"I suggest we follow Stuart's example, just to get our bearings," Forbee-X said. "We can make wider and wider circles to explore the terrain."

Artoo began to roll away, and Threepio followed him. Artoo chirped and beeped.

"Yes, it does seem deserted," Threepio said. "I don't know what frightens me more — running across life-forms, or finding nobody at all."

But after a long, dusty walk, Artoo and Threepio still hadn't found any trace of intelligent life-forms. Discouraged, they trudged back to the pod, where they found Forbee-X waiting.

"Where's Stuart?" Forbee-X asked worriedly. "It will be getting dark soon."

"We didn't see Master Stuart," Threepio replied. "I hope he isn't lost."

But a moment later, Stuart ran up to them, out of breath. "I've been climbing the ridge," he said, pointing in the distance. "I thought I'd be able to see that city."

"That wasn't a city," Threepio said, shaking his head.

"But I forgot to take the macrobinoculars," Stuart finished. "I'll go see if I can find them."

"But you don't have time to go back to the ridge!" Forbee-X called after him. "We'd better talk him out of it," she said to Threepio and Artoo. "Darkness is falling too rapidly."

They all hurried back to the pod. When they climbed inside, they found Stuart rooting through the equipment that had fallen on the floor during the landing.

"What's this?" he asked, holding up a small black box.

"It's a data recorder, I believe," Threepio said.

Stuart pushed a button. Suddenly, Princess Leia's voice filled the cabin.

"*Greetings, Governor Zissu. If you are listening to this, it means our plan was successful. You have abandoned the* Timespan *and are on your way to*

Romm to hook up with the Rebel faction. You know the coordinates of the site. It won't be an easy journey, but I know that you will succeed.

"If we are right, the Imperials will assume that the Timespan *malfunctioned and you left for the nearest planet, Benon. That should buy you time.*

"As for Stuart, he —"

Suddenly, static took over the transmission. Stuart tried several buttons, then tried shaking the recorder, but the rest of the transmission was lost.

"How extraordinary," Threepio said. "We were *supposed* to leave the *Timespan*. But apparently, the Imperials boarded us before we got the chance."

Artoo whirred and clicked.

"Yes, that's most likely why Captain Solo made sure the pod had special features," Threepio agreed. "But the plan certainly went awry."

"I wonder what Princess Leia was going to say about me," Stuart said.

"There must be an Imperial spy on Yavin 4," Forbee-X said. "Obviously, the Imperials knew exactly where we'd be. And if they sabotaged the pod, they knew what the plan was. Just in case they weren't able to capture Governor Zissu, they made sure he would have trouble reaching Romm. That's the only logical conclusion."

Artoo beeped, and Threepio nodded.

"Artoo thinks that the Rebels on Romm must be

in danger, too," he explained. "But the princess was careful not to give the coordinates of their position."

Stuart suddenly turned pale. "That's why they captured Father! They need those coordinates!"

Threepio sank down on the gee-couch. "This is getting terribly serious. We have to find a way off this planet. We must tell Princess Leia about the spy!"

"Artoo, can you try to fix the comm transceiver again?" Forbee-X suggested. One arm extended and plucked a small container from the pile of debris on the floor. "Look, a repair kit spilled out with the emergency supplies. Maybe something in here could help."

Artoo beeped excitedly once he saw what was in the kit. He rolled over to the transceiver. A series of whistles told Threepio that Artoo was pleased with his progress.

"I think he can fix it!" Threepio said excitedly.

Static filled the air. Artoo quickly made some adjustments. He beeped at the unit, and it answered in a series of beeps.

"He's entering Leia's secret emergency code," Threepio explained to Forbee-X and Stuart. "I hope this works! The princess will tell us exactly what to do."

Suddenly, through the static, they heard the faint voice of the princess.

"This is Princess Leia. Is that you, Artoo? Do you copy?"

Threepio sprang forward. "Yes, it's us, Princess Leia! We don't know where we are, but we're on some planet in the Delantine system. Commander Zissu has been captured!"

"Tell her about the spy!" Stuart called.

"And there's a spy on Yavin 4!" Threepio yelled. "Do you copy?"

There was a burst of static. "I copy," Princess Leia said. "But I'm losing the transmission. Find the nearest settlement. Repeat: find the nearest settlement. You only have a short amount of time. Get there *now*. I have ordered evacuation of all Rebel forces in the Delantine system. You have forty-eight hours to make contact. I will alert Rebel factions to be on the watch."

"Yes, Princess," Threepio said. "I mean, I copy."

More static drowned out Princess Leia's voice.

"What was that? We didn't read," Threepio spoke into the comm unit. "Repeat."

"Rescue mission," Princess Leia said. More static drowned out her voice again. "Romm."

Suddenly, her voice was cut off. Artoo tried to fix the unit, but it was broken for good.

"Did you hear that?" Stuart said, springing forward. "The princess wants us to lead a rescue mission. First, we have to contact the Rebel base on Romm."

"I didn't hear that at all," Threepio disagreed. "We missed half of what she said. She could have said that they will launch a rescue mission from Romm to rescue us, as well as your father."

"Let's start with what we *do* know," Forbee-X said. "The princess told us to go to the nearest settlement. *Quickly.* So that's what we'll do. We can argue about what to do next once we get there."

Stuart grabbed the macrobinoculars. "I'm going to hike to that far ridge," he said. His green eyes shone with grim determination. "We can start tonight. We have to get to Romm. It's our only hope. We can make contact with the Rebels and rescue Father!"

Stuart ran down the ramp, and Forbee-X quickly wheeled after him. Threepio and Artoo followed.

"Stuart, stop!" she called in a commanding voice. "You must listen to me!"

Reluctantly, Stuart turned.

"Look around you," Forbee-X urged. "It's going to be dark soon. You'll never find your way."

"I can bring a glow rod," Stuart said stubbornly.

"And the temperature has fallen rapidly," Forbee-X continued. Her blue screen flashed with data.

"It *is* getting chilly," Threepio agreed. "And look

at that tree. I could have sworn it had green leaves. Now they're bright red. I must have been mistaken."

Forbee-X's screen filled up with formulas and numbers. They flashed so quickly Threepio couldn't read them.

"I've analyzed the additional data," Forbee-X said. "It doesn't compute, but it is fact. Very strange."

"Oh, dear. That doesn't sound very reassuring," Threepio said.

Artoo beeped and whistled, then chirped.

"Artoo thinks the best thing to do is to camp for the night, and then start off in the morning," Threepio told them.

"I agree," Forbee-X said. "I don't like these readings."

"But we have to rescue Father!" Stuart burst out. "We can't waste any time!"

"Stuart, this is the best we can do," Forbee-X said gently. "We need daylight to explore. What if we go the wrong way? It could waste precious time."

Stuart looked as though he wanted to run off. His whole body tensed. Then his shoulders slumped. "I guess I don't have a choice."

Forbee-X's arm extended and she hooked a hand around his shoulder gently. "We're in this together, Stuart."

"We'll find a way to rescue your father," Threepio

told him. "If we have to go to Romm, we will." He felt very brave making the promise.

Artoo beeped in agreement.

"Let's make camp," Forbee-X suggested. "Stuart needs rest. Who knows what tomorrow will bring."

Threepio gazed at his surroundings. It was almost dark now. As he watched, the tree nearest them suddenly dropped all its red leaves at once.

They all exchanged stunned glances.

"Tomorrow? I don't even want to think about it," Threepio moaned.

STAR WARS SCIENCE ACTIVITIES
Experiments for your own world

1. Centrifugal Force

How did centrifugal force plaster Stuart and the droids to the walls of the pod? Try it yourself as you take an action figure for a wild ride.

Materials:
action figure
umbrella
wide, open space

1. Open an umbrella and hold it upside down. Drop an action figure inside. Turn it right side up. What happens? The force of gravity pulls the action figure out of the umbrella. In other words, the figure falls.

2. Put the figure back inside the umbrella. This time, apply some centrifugal force by swinging the umbrella in a big circle.

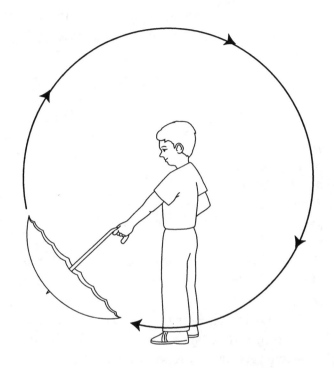

What happens this time?

- **If the figure stayed in the umbrella,** the centrifugal force you made was stronger than gravity.
- **If the action figure fell,** the centrifugal force you made was weaker than gravity. Swing the umbrella faster next time.

2. Rocket Fuel

How could two chemicals mix together to make fuel for the escape pod? Power a palm-sized rocket to find out.

Materials

empty film canister
1 tsp vinegar
½ tsp baking soda
safety goggles
adult partner
old clothes

1. Put on some old clothes, grab an adult partner, and head outside. (This is messy!) Put on your safety goggles.
2. Pour 1 tsp vinegar into an empty film canister.
3. Spoon out ½ tsp baking soda. Don't put it in the canister yet! But get ready to act fast.
4. *Quickly* pour the baking soda into the canister.
5. *Quickly* push the cover tightly onto the canister. (Use your palm to press it down.)
6. *Quickly* turn the canister upside down on the ground.
7. Stand back — the canister is about to go flying! What makes it go sky-high? A chemical reaction. That's when two substances combine to form

an entirely new substance. (And sometimes two or more.)

When the baking soda hit the vinegar, a chemical reaction between the two created bubbles of carbon dioxide gas. As the gas built up in the canister, it pressed on the lid. When the pressure got too great — POP! The canister blew its top.

3. Thrusters

How could firing the escape pod's thrusters make it spin out of control? Give this experiment a whirl to find out.

Materials

paper plate
string
pen
tape
two long balloons

1. Use a pen to poke a hole in the middle of the plate. (To find the middle: Try to balance the plate on your finger. When the plate is well balanced, your finger is in the middle.)
2. Thread the string through the hole.
3. Tape each end of the string to a table or chair. Make sure the string is fairly tight.
4. Make two tape loops, sticky side out. Place

them on the same side of the plate, but opposite each other, as shown.

Step 4

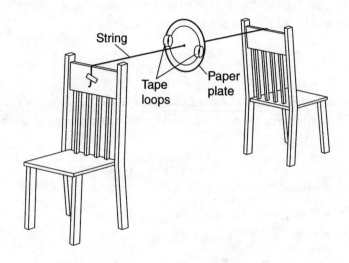

5. Blow up one of the balloons. Hold the neck of the first balloon closed while you blow up the second. (Or have a partner blow up the second balloon.)

6. Keep holding both balloon necks closed. Hold one balloon with the neck pointed down and stick it to the tape loop on the left. Hold the other balloon with the neck pointed up and stick it to the tape loop on the right.

7. Let go of both balloon necks at once, and

stand back. What happens? How is this like the thrusters and the spinning escape pod?

8. You just simulated firing the two thrusters circled below. How could you use the balloons and plate to test different combinations of thrusters?

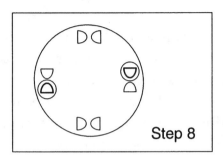

Step 8

SCIENCE FACTS FOR USE ON EARTH

It's the Law!

• The First Law of Motion, as explained by Forbee-X (p. 22), is valid in our galaxy as well. On Earth, it was discovered more than 300 years ago by Sir Isaac Newton. It was the first of Newton's Three Laws of Motion. Newton's Laws say that all objects, from marbles to ships to planets, follow the same basic set of rules. Sir Isaac Newton was a busy guy. The Englishman also explained gravity, built the first reflecting telescope, and invented a kind of math called calculus.

• When you skateboard, you prove Newton's First Law. Here's how: Launch yourself forward, and your board will keep going in the same direction until a force acts on it — for instance, your leaning to the right or left. Your board will also keep up the same speed until a force acts on it, and one force always does — friction. The friction (rubbing) between your board's wheels and axles, as well as the friction between your wheels and the ground, work to slow the board down. That's why you have to keep pumping with your foot. By the way, Newton's First Law also says that a body at rest stays at rest until a force acts on it. You prove that law every time you park your board in a corner overnight, and pick it up in the exact same spot the next morning.

• You can get a feel for high and low gravity (p. 32) by hopping on an elevator. (The faster the ride, the better.) Get on at the first floor and press the top button. After the doors shut, close your eyes and concentrate. The "heavy" feeling you get as the elevator car starts to head up is like high gravity. The "lift" you feel as the car stops at the top is like low gravity.

Deep (and Not So Deep) Impact

• Want to navigate an asteroid field? In our solar system, you can head to the asteroid belt, a ring of rocks located between the orbits of Mars and Jupiter. Many of the asteroids there are miles wide, so you'll want to pay attention to the viewscreen. The asteroids are far apart, so you probably won't need to copy Stuart's tricky steering moves (p. 50). Make sure your craft has full shields, though. The belt has tons of pint-sized asteroids that would be hard to spot and steer around — but solid enough to punch a hole in a speeding spacecraft.

• Because orbit is a perfect balance between gravity and the spacecraft's forward motion, the space shuttle actually falls around Earth. That free fall is what makes the astronauts feel weightless. But gravity still affects them. It's what keeps them from shooting away from the planet in a straight line (p. 52).

• Space probes "slingshot" around planets (p. 53) in order to pick up speed and change direction.

• Earth's atmosphere (p. 59) fades into space about 180 miles above the planet's surface, but most of the clouds and weather stay in the lowest seven miles of the atmosphere, in a layer called the troposphere.

• When Apollo astronauts reentered Earth's atmosphere, they used parachutes to create drag and slow down their command modules. When today's astronauts come back to Earth, they use the shuttle itself to create drag. That friction between the shuttle and the air creates a lot of heat. Parts of the shuttle's outer surface rise to a sizzling 2,500°F. The astronauts inside, however, don't even break a sweat. They're protected by special heat-blocking tiles on the shuttle's hull.